FOR MY DAUGHTER ASHLEY

NORMAN ROCKWELL'S

Diary For a Young Girl

WITH VERSE BY

GEORGE MENDOZA

ABBEVILLE PRESS, INC.,
PUBLISHERS

ISBN 0-89659-013-5

NORMAN ROCKWELL'S

Diary For a Young Girl

I am your diary to keep forever
  a marker for your most secret secrets...
Your place to go when you feel alone
  with your feelings...

I am your head in the clouds

and your dreams asail...

I am your adventures

on your way over the mountains...

I am the day you will never forget...

*I am your Little Prince you promised
to love always...*

Birthday
Miss Jones
Suprise
happy
Surprise
surprise
birth
to Miss Jo
Jonesy
Happy Birth
Teache

I am the memories of happy birthdays...

Courtesy of Parker Pen Company

I am all your love for your father...

I am your thoughts
when you look up at your mother...

I am a
golden locket
waiting to be
opened and closed...

NORMAN ROCKWELL

I am like a sea shell spinning

mysteries,

press me close and I'll whisper

back to you...

I am the time of your life,
all your joys
and all your tomorrows...

I am your seasons

Springtime

of wonder...

I am what you want to be

when you grow up...

Most of all,
I am a garden
for your dreams,
a place to grow
your stars and flowers...

I am as close to your heart

as you are to mine...

I am like the silence of

the snowy woods...

I am the poems you write
when you are alone...

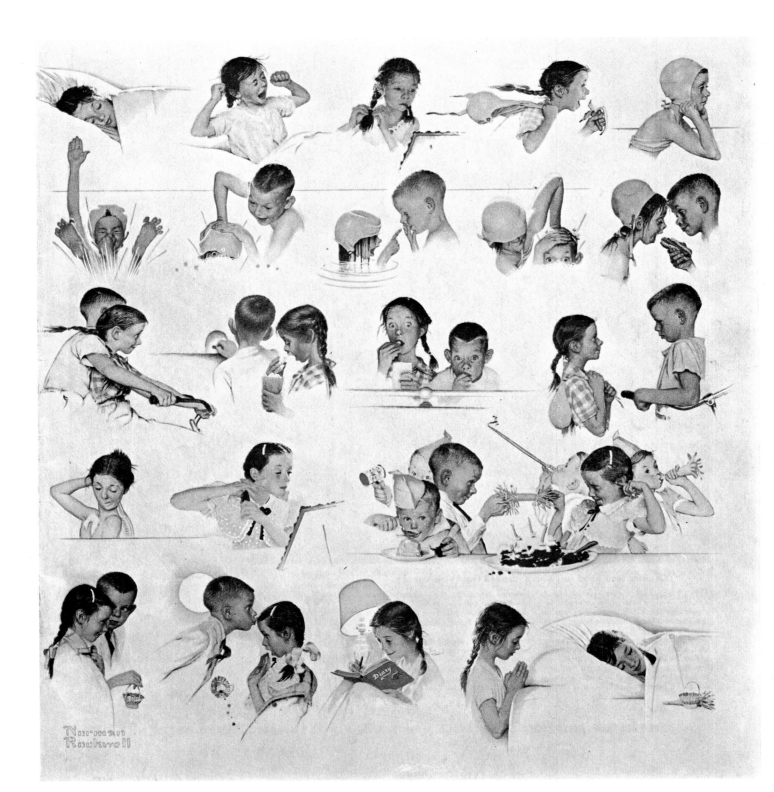

I am school days and holidays,
a windmill of memories...

I am your deepest secrets
you can tell only to me...

*I am a store full
of hidden surprises*

for you to discover within youself...

I am like a bird flying with clouds...

I am sometimes a sad note;
I'll help you write it away...

I am your first love letter you will never send...

I am a traceless track of names

you will remember forever...

I am your secrets and that means...

NAME	ADDRESS	TELEPHONE
Bill Platt "Pookes"	RR #3 Thorton	737-4658
Diana Acheson "Ach"	213 Younge	436-1318
Lisa Duivenvoorden "Doove"	RR #1 Stroud	436-1046

NAME	ADDRESS	TELEPHONE

NAME	ADDRESS	TELEPHONE

NAME	ADDRESS	TELEPHONE

NAME	ADDRESS	TELEPHONE

NAME	ADDRESS	TELEPHONE

NAME	ADDRESS	TELEPHONE

NAME	ADDRESS	TELEPHONE

An Extra Seat

By Rabbi Shmuel Herzfeld

Illustrations: J.B. & C.B. Herzfeld

gefen גפן
publishing house בית תוצאה לאור
JERUSALEM • NEW YORK   Est. 1981

Design: Virtual Paintbrush
Edited by Amanda Cohen

ISBN: 978-965-229-873-7

1 3 5 7 9 8 6 4 2

Gefen Publishing House Ltd.
6 Hatzvi Street
Jerusalem 94386, Israel
972-2-538-0247
orders@gefenpublishing.com

Gefen Books
11 Edison Place
Springfield, NJ 07081
516-593-1234
orders@gefenpublishing.com

www.gefenpublishing.com

Printed in Israel

Library of Congress Cataloging-in-Publication Data

Names: Herzfeld, Shmuel, author. | Benjamin, Amanda, contributor. | Herzfeld, Caryl, illustrator.
Title: An extra seat / by Rabbi Shmuel Herzfeld ; with Amanda Benjamin ; [illustrations by Caryl Herzfeld].
Description: Jerusalem, Israel ; Springfield, NJ : Gefen Publishing House, [2016]. | Summary: "Inspired by
their rabbi, Sarah and David add their voices to the the unjust imprisonment of Soviet Jew, Natan Sharansky,
remembering and honoring him in their own unique way, while discovering that to follow one's heart with
action brings its own deep reward"-- Provided by publisher.
Identifiers: LCCN 2016004141 | ISBN 9789652298737
Subjects: | CYAC: Shcharansky, Anatoly--Fiction. | Jews--Soviet Union--Fiction. | Jews--Fiction. |
Rabbis--Fiction. | Brothers and sisters--Fiction.
Classification: LCC PZ7.1.H496 Ex 2016 | DDC [Fic]--dc23 LC record available at
https://lccn.loc.gov/2016004141

Dedication

This book is dedicated to the memory of Dr. David Gitler, *z"l*. Through his medical practice, Dr. Gitler was passionately dedicated to treating all of his patients with dignity.

As a doctor in Camp Tagola he also had the privilege of living next door to Rabbi Avi Weiss, whom he respected tremendously for his dedication to relieving pain and suffering throughout the world and especially his work on behalf of the Prisoners of Zion. Some of his proudest moments as a father came from being able to witness the work that his children did for Jews around the world, including Jews in the former Soviet Union.

May his memory be a blessing!

The Gitler Family

It was 1977.

A young rabbi in New York named Avi Weiss was speaking to his congregation one Shabbat morning after the services were over, about some

very

brave

Jews.

Two children, called Sarah and Joseph, listened carefully.

Far away, in the Soviet Union,

a group of Jews had tried to leave to find a better life in Israel.
They were not allowed to. In fact, they were punished
for trying to leave - as if a

GIANT
IRON
DOOR

was closed in their faces.

One of those courageous Jews was called Anatoly Sharansky.
He had just been arrested.

"Sharansky is our brother,"

Rabbi Weiss told his congregation passionately.
"Let's all rally tomorrow to support him,
and say, 'Let my people go!' just like Moses did
when he led the Israelites out of slavery in Egypt."

Afterwards, Joseph asked his parents if they could all go to the rally the next day.

"Yes," they answered him. "But the USSR is very far away –

they probably don't care what we say or do."

Sarah went up to Rabbi Weiss. "Why did you call Sharansky my brother? I've never even met him. Joseph is my brother!"

Rabbi Weiss smiled.
"We care deeply about
all human beings, but we have
the greatest responsibility to help
our own family. All of the Jewish
people are one family. Like the Torah says,

"We are all responsible to help each other.""

The next day, Sarah and Joseph marched in New York, alongside their rabbi. Holding signs that read, "Free Sharansky!" they chanted,

"One, two, three, four, open up the Iron Door! Five, six, seven, eight, we don't want to wait!"

That night,

they watched the news on TV.
There was Rabbi Weiss, pleading
for the release of Sharansky!
But there was no news of Sharansky.
He was still in jail – waiting to be
sentenced or set free. The children felt
very sad, but they continued to raise
a voice on his behalf when they could.

Then one day they heard the terrible news. Sharansky had been sentenced to thirteen years in jail! Sarah started to cry.

"What was the point?" she asked Rabbi Weiss. "They don't care what we say or do."

Rabbi Weiss spoke softly to her. "We will just have to work harder and keep on trying.

Let's see what else we can do for our brother."

The following week was Sarah's birthday.
She set an extra chair at the table.

She told everyone:

"This is a seat for Sharansky.

Even as we celebrate, we have to remember
those who don't get to have fun."

Sarah's friends started setting an extra seat at
their tables for Sharansky, too - for Shabbat
dinners and holiday celebrations.

"You know, there are other prisoners suffering as much as Sharansky," Joseph told his school friends.

"Joseph Mendelevitch. Ida Nudel."

Then he had an idea. "Let's all wear a silver bracelet engraved with the name of a Prisoner of Zion. This way, we will always be thinking about them and others will see us supporting them."

Soon every child in Joseph's school wore a bracelet with the name of a Jewish prisoner on it.

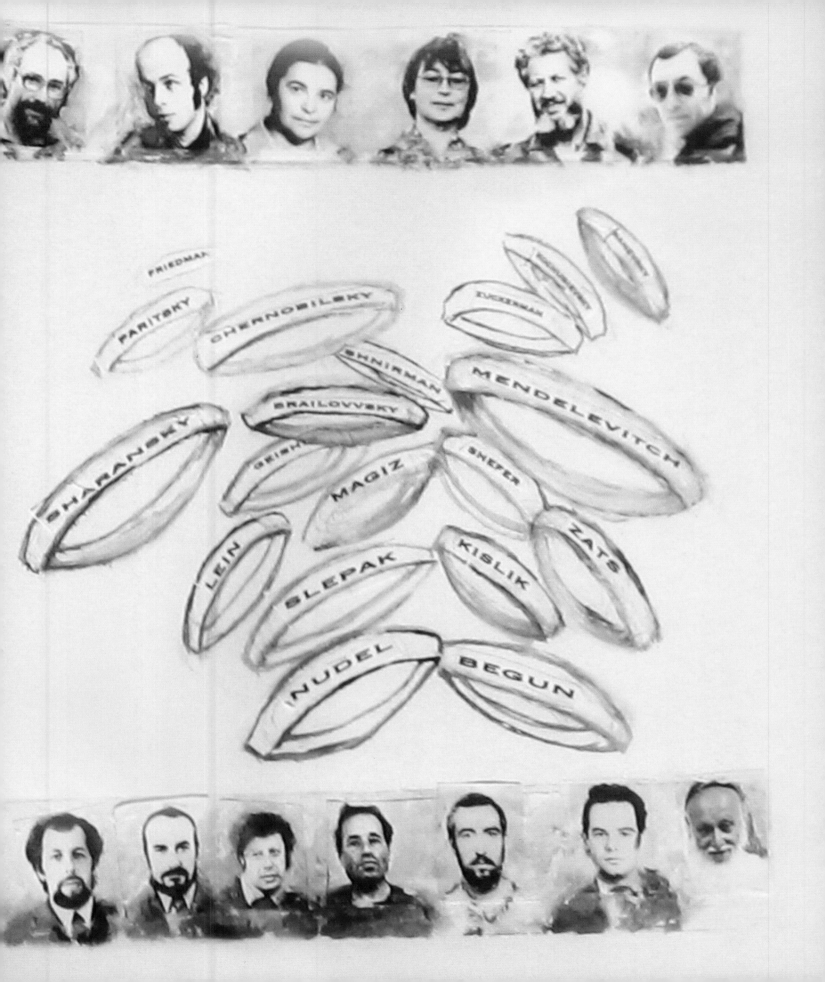

One Shabbat morning, a very special visitor came to Sarah and Joseph's synagogue -

Avital, Sharansky's wife.

She had managed leave the USSR before he was arrested. Now she traveled the world, telling people about the Jews stuck in the USSR, and

how they desperately needed help.

After services,

Sarah went up to Avital and gave her

a big hug.

She told how she had set a place for her husband at her birthday party. Avital smiled. "Hearing that would make him very happy," she said.

Avital told them all that her husband was refusing to eat,

in protest.

Rabbi Weiss immediately said:

"My friends, I am also going on a hunger strike!

To show the world how much we care about our brothers and sisters

in the USSR."

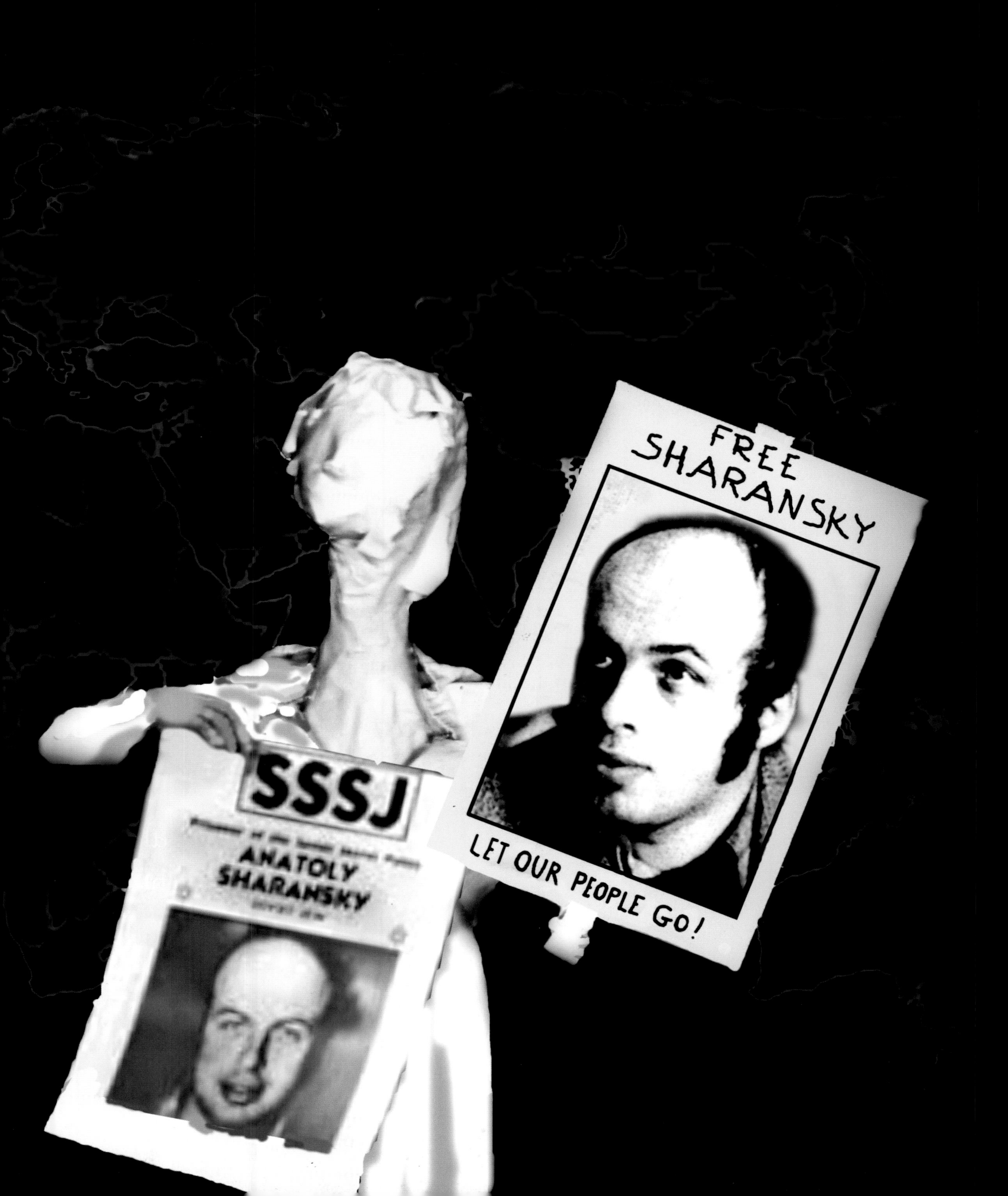
SSSJ
ANATOLY
SHARANSKY
FREE
SHARANSKY
LET OUR PEOPLE GO!

Then one Shabbat morning in 1983, Rabbi Weiss rallied everyone together again –

for a huge protest

in front of the United Nations. Joseph knew what he had to do.

After Havdalah, he called all of his friends, his grandparents and cousins, and even his teachers. "Please come tomorrow," he begged. "We all need to help free Sharansky!"

The next day, tens of thousands gathered in the streets
of New York. There were people from all religions.
There were congressmen and senators. The mayor
of New York City came! Rabbi Weiss cried out:

"Let my people go!
Free Sharansky now!"

Everyone raised their voices together,
"*Am Yisrael chai*, the Jewish people
will live!" Surely their voices
would be heard!

The fight to free
Sharansky went
on year after year.

Joseph and Sarah grew busy with school and friends and they sometimes felt ready to give up. But how could they when Sharansky was still in prison? When Rabbi Weiss wasn't giving up?

Then one day in 1986, they heard the amazing news.

Sharansky had been freed!

Joseph, now a teenager, was so happy that he started to cry. Full of joy, Sarah hugged her mother tightly.

The fight had taken nine years. Sharansky would join Avital in Israel. He had changed his name to the Hebrew: "Natan".

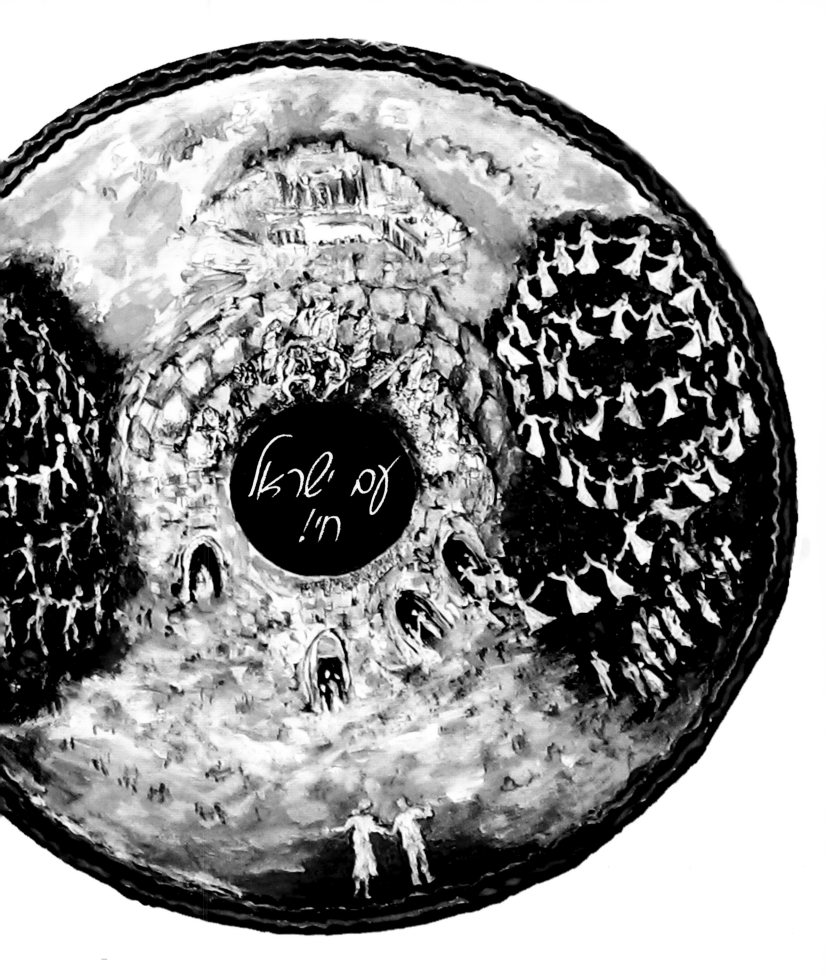

Soon after, Rabbi Weiss told them something very exciting.

Sharansky was coming to their synagogue!

Joseph and Sarah
could hardly wait.

THIS SEAT IS RESERVED FOR SHARANSKY

"Thank you for all your work to help me," Sharansky told them all. "I never felt alone! But we can't stop now. There are other people to help."

Joseph and Sarah sat up front,

listening to every word.

Sharansky told them a story:

"The prison guards tried to make me feel bad. They'd say,
'No one cares about you. You are all alone!'

But I knew it wasn't true.

Then one day they showed me a picture of people at a rally for me. 'See!' they taunted. 'The only ones who care about you are students and children.'"

He smiled. "They wanted to break my spirit. But when they showed me that picture, it made me so happy.

When children care about something, they can be stronger than even a big country like the USSR."

Joseph and Sarah ran up to Rabbi Weiss.

"Thank you for never giving up hope," he told them.

"Without your help, Natan would still be in prison. You know, the rabbis tell us something very important.

'It is not our responsibility to complete the task, but we are obligated to try!'"

Author's Note

Shmuel Herzfeld was born in 1974 and raised in Staten Island, New York. He traveled regularly with his family to Sunday rallies in New York City on behalf of Soviet Jewry, and also on multiple occasions to larger rallies in Washington, DC. As a young child he proudly wore the names of Prisoners of Zion on bracelets. Later he served as assistant rabbi at the Hebrew Institute of Riverdale, where Rabbi Avi Weiss was the senior rabbi. There he heard many stories from congregants about Rabbi Weiss who, along with so many others in the Jewish community, worked tirelessly on behalf of Soviet Jewry as part of the Student Struggle for Soviet Jewry. This story reminds us that children have the power to change the world through their idealism and activism.